S0-AJR-238

TALES OF PETER RABBIT

TALES OF PETER RABBIT

BY
BEATRIX POTTER

ILLUSTRATIONS BY
CHARLES SANTORE

RUNNING PRESS BOOK PUBLISHERS
PHILADELPHIA, PENNSYLVANIA

Canadian representatives: General Publishing Co.,
Ltd., 30 Lesmill Road, Don Mills, Ontario M3B 2T6.
International representatives: Worldwide Media
Services, Inc., 115 East Twenty-third Street, New York,
NY 10010.
9 8 7 6 5 4 3 2 1
Digit on the right indicates the number of this printing.
Library of Congress Catalog Card Number: 91-52695
ISBN 1-56138-039-3
This book may be ordered by mail from the publisher.
Please add $2.50 for postage and handling. *But try your
bookstore first!*
Running Press Book Publishers
125 South Twenty-second Street
Philadelphia, Pennsylvania 19103

CONTENTS

INTRODUCTION

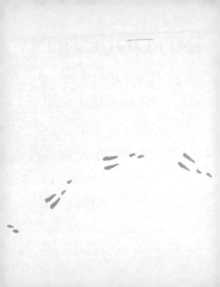

Born in London in 1866, Beatrix Potter began her writing career at the age of 27. Her first story was written as an illustrated letter to a sick child, and featured her mischievous pet rabbit, Peter.

The Tale of Peter Rabbit was first published in 1900. From that time until her death in 1943, Beatrix Potter continued to write and illustrate her stories, leaving to the world's children a legacy of

closely observed and
charming tales.

In this volume, ac-
claimed illustrator
Charles Santore brings a
new vision to Beatrix
Potter's work. These 49
full-color and exquisitely
detailed illustrations

invite you to explore the
world as seen through
the eyes of Peter, his
family, and his friends.

A freshly illustrated
presentation of three
familiar texts, this edi-
tion of *Tales of Peter*
Rabbit is a lasting

addition to the legacy of
Beatrix Potter.

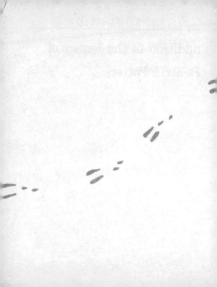

THE TALE OF
PETER RABBIT

Once upon a time there
were four little Rabbits,
and their names were—
Flopsy,
Mopsy,
Cotton-tail,
and Peter.

They lived with their
mother in a sand-bank,

underneath the root of a
very big fir-tree.

"Now, my dears," said
old Mrs. Rabbit one
morning, "you may go
into the fields or down
the lane, but don't go into
Mr. McGregor's garden:
your father had an acci-
dent there; he was put in
a pie by Mrs. McGregor."

Then old Mrs. Rabbit took a basket and her umbrella, and went through the wood to the baker's. She bought a loaf of brown bread and five currant buns.

Flopsy, Mopsy, and Cotton-tail, who were good little bunnies, went down the lane to gather

blackberries: but Peter,
who was very naughty,
ran straight away to Mr.
McGregor's garden,
and

squeezed

under the gate!

First he ate some
lettuces and some French
beans; and
then

he ate some radishes;
but round the end of a
cucumber frame,
whom should
he meet
but...

Mr. McGregor!

Mr. McGregor was on his hands and knees planting out young cabbages, but he jumped up and ran after Peter, waving a rake and calling out, "Stop thief!"

Peter was most dreadfully frightened; he rushed all over the garden, for he had forgotten the way back to the gate.

He lost one of his shoes among the cabbages, and the other shoe amongst the potatoes.

After losing them, he ran on four legs and went

faster, so that I think he
might have got away
altogether if he had not
unfortunately run into a
gooseberry net, and got
caught by the large
buttons on his jacket. It
was a blue jacket with
brass buttons, quite new.

Peter gave himself up
for lost, and shed big

tears; but his sobs were over-heard by some friendly sparrows, who flew to him in great excitement, and implored him to exert himself.

Mr. McGregor came up with a sieve, which he intended to pop upon the top of Peter; but Peter wriggled out just in time, leaving his jacket behind him, and rushed into the tool-shed, and jumped into a can. It would have been a beautiful thing to

hide in, if it had not had
so much water in it.

Mr. McGregor was quite sure that Peter was somewhere in the toolshed, perhaps hidden underneath a flower-pot. He began to turn them over carefully, looking under each.

Presently Peter sneezed—"Kertyschoo!" Mr. McGregor was after

him in no time, and tried
to put his foot upon Peter,
who jumped
out
of a
window,

upsetting
three
plants.

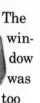

The
win-
dow
was
too

small for Mr. McGregor,
and he was tired of

running after Peter. He
went back to his work.

Peter sat down to rest;
he was out of breath and
trembling with fright,
and he had not the least
idea which way to go.
Also he was very damp
with sitting in that can.

After a time he began
to wander about, going

lippity—

lippity—not very
fast, and looking all
around.

He found a door in a
wall; but it was locked,
and there was no room for
a fat little rabbit to
squeeze underneath.

An old mouse was
running in and out over

the stone doorstep,
carrying peas and beans
to her family in the wood.

Peter
asked
her
the
way
to

the gate, but she had
such a large pea in her
mouth that she could not
answer. She only shook
her head at him. Peter
began to cry.

Then he tried to find
his way straight
across the garden,
but he became more
and more puzzled.

Presently, he came to a
pond where Mr. McGregor
filled his water-
cans. A
white cat
was staring
at some
goldfish;
she sat
very,
very still,

but now and then the tip of her tail twitched as if it were alive. Peter thought it best to go away without speaking to her; he had heard about cats from his cousin, little Benjamin Bunny.

He went back

towards the tool-shed,
but suddenly, quite close
to him, he heard the
noise of a hoe—

scr-r-ritch,

scratch,

scratch,

scritch.

Peter scuttered under-
neath the bushes. But
presently, as nothing

41

happened, he came out, and climbed upon a wheelbarrow and peeped over. The first thing he saw was Mr. McGregor hoeing onions. His back was turned towards Peter, and beyond him was the gate!

Peter got down very quietly off the wheelbar-

row, and started running
as fast as he could go,
along a straight walk
behind some black-
currant bushes.

Mr. McGregor caught
sight of him at the corner,
but Peter did
not care. He
slipped under-
neath the gate,

43

and was safe at last in
the wood outside the
garden.

Mr. McGregor hung
up the little jacket and

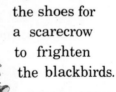

the shoes for
a scarecrow
to frighten
the blackbirds.

Peter never stopped running or looked behind him till he got home to the big fir-tree.

He was so tired that he flopped down upon the nice soft sand on the floor of the rabbit hole and shut his eyes. His mother was busy cooking; she wondered what he had done with his clothes. It was the second little jacket and pair of shoes that Peter had lost in a fortnight!

I am sorry to say that Peter was not very well during the evening.

His mother put him to bed, and made some camomile tea; and she

gave a dose of it to Peter!
   "One tablespoonful to

be taken at bedtime."

But Flopsy, Mopsy, and Cotton-tail had bread and milk and blackberries for supper.

THE TALE OF
BENJAMIN
BUNNY

One morning a little
rabbit sat on a bank. He
pricked his ears and
listened to the

      trit-trot,

         trit-trot

            of a pony.

A gig was coming
along the road; it was
driven by Mr. McGregor,

and beside him sat Mrs. McGregor in her best bonnet.

As soon as they had passed, little Benjamin Bunny slid down into the road, and set off—with a h^op, s k i p and a j u m p— to call upon his relations, who lived in the wood at the back of Mr. McGregor's garden.

That wood was full of rabbit holes; and in the neatest sandiest hole of all, lived Benjamin's aunt and his cousins—Flopsy, Mopsy, Cotton-tail and Peter.

Old Mrs. Rabbit was a widow; she earned her

living by knitting rabbit-
wool mittens and
muffetees (I once bought
a pair at a bazaar). She
also sold herbs, and
rosemary tea, and rabbit-
tobacco (which is what *we*
call lavender).

Little Benjamin
did not

very much want to see
his aunt.

He came round the
back of the fir-tree, and
nearly tumbled upon the
top of his cousin Peter.

Peter was sitting by
himself. He looked poorly,
and was dressed in a

red cotton pocket-handkerchief.

"Peter,"—said little Benjamin, in a whisper—"who has got your clothes?"

Peter replied—"The scarecrow in Mr. McGregor's garden,"

 and described how he had been chased about the garden, and had dropped his shoes and coat.

Little Benjamin sat down beside his cousin, and assured him that Mr. McGregor had gone out in a gig, and Mrs. McGregor also; and certainly for the day, because she was wearing her best bonnet.

Peter said he hoped that it would rain.

At this point, old Mrs. Rabbit's voice was heard inside the rabbit hole, calling—"Cotton-tail!

Cotton-tail! fetch
some more camomile!"
Peter said he
thought he might feel
better if he went for a
walk.

They went away hand in hand, and got upon the flat top of the wall at the bottom of the wood. From here they looked down into Mr. McGregor's garden. Peter's coat and shoes were plainly to be seen upon the scarecrow, topped with an old tam-o-shanter of Mr. McGregor's.

Little Benjamin said, "It spoils people's clothes to squeeze under a gate; the proper way to get in, is to climb down a pear tree."

Peter fell do_{w_n}

head first; but it was of
no consequence, as the
bed below was newly
raked and quite soft.

It had been sown with
lettuces.

They left a great many
odd little

65

footmarks all over the bed, especially little Benjamin, who was wearing clogs.

Little Benjamin said that the first thing to be done was to get back Peter's clothes, in order that they might be able to use the pocket-handkerchief.

They took them off the scarecrow. There had been rain during the night; there was water in the shoes, and the coat was some-what shrunk.

Benjamin tried on the tam-o-shanter, but it was too **big**

for him.

Then he suggested that they should fill the pocket-handkerchief with onions, as a little present for his aunt.

Peter did not seem to be enjoying himself; he kept hearing noises.

Benjamin, on the contrary, was perfectly at

home,
and ate
a lettuce
leaf. He said that he was
in the habit of coming to
the garden with his
father to get lettuces for
their Sunday dinner.

(The name of little
Benjamin's papa was old
Mr. Benjamin Bunny.)

The lettuces certainly were very fine.

Peter did not eat anything; he said he should like to go home. Presently he dropped half the onions.

Little Benjamin said that it was not possible to get back up the pear tree, with a load of vegetables. He led the way boldly

towards the other end of
the garden.

They went along a
little walk on planks,
under a sunny red-
brick wall.

The mice sat on
their doorsteps
cracking cherry-
stones;
they

71

winked at
Peter Rab-
bit and
little

Benjamin
Bunny.
Presently
Peter let the
pocket-handker-
chief go again.
They got amongst

72

flower-pots, and frames and tubs. Peter heard noises worse than ever; his eyes were as big as lolly-pops!

He was a step or two in front of his cousin, when he suddenly stopped.

This is what those little rabbits saw round that corner!

THE TALE OF BENJAMIN BUNNY

Little Benjamin took
one look, and then, in
half a minute less than
no time, he hid himself
and Peter and the onions
underneath a large
basket. . . .

The cat got up and
s t r e t c h e d
herself, and came and
sniffed at the basket.

Perhaps she liked the smell of onions!

Anyway, she sat down upon the top of the basket.

She sat there for *five hours*.

I cannot draw you a picture of Peter and Benjamin underneath the basket, because it was quite dark, and because the smell of onions was fearful; it make Peter Rabbit and little Benjamin cry.

The sun got round behind the wood, and it was quite late in the after-noon; but still

the cat sat upon the
basket.

At length there was a
pitter-patter,

pitter-patter,
and some bits of mortar
fell from the wall above.

The cat looked up and
saw old Mr. Benjamin
Bunny prancing along
the top of the wall of the

upper terrace.

He was smoking a pipe of rabbit-tobacco, and had a little switch in his hand.

He was looking for his son.

Old Mr. Bunny had no opinion whatever of cats.

He took a tremendous jump off the top of the

wall on to the
top of the cat,
and cuffed it
off the basket,
and kicked it
into the

green-house, scratching
off a handful of fur.

The cat was too much
surprised to scratch back.

When old Mr. Bunny
had driven the cat into
the green-house, he
locked the door.

Then he came back to
the basket and took out
his son Benjamin by the

ears, and whipped him with the little switch.

Then he took out his nephew Peter.

Then he took out the handkerchief of onions, and marched out of the garden.

When Mr. McGregor returned about half an hour later, he observed

several things which
perplexed him.

It looked as though
some person had been
walking all over the
garden in a pair of clogs—
only the footmarks were
too ridiculously little!

Also he could not

understand how the cat
could have managed to
shut herself up *inside* the
green-house, locking the
door upon the *outside*.

When Peter got home,
his mother forgave him,
because she was so glad
to see that he had found
his shoes and coat.
Cotton-tail and Peter

folded up the pocket-
handkerchief, and old

Mrs. Rabbit strung up the onions and hung them from the kitchen ceiling, with the bunches of herbs and the rabbit-tobacco.

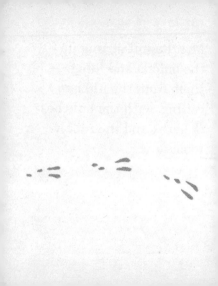

THE TALE OF
THE FLOPSY
BUNNIES

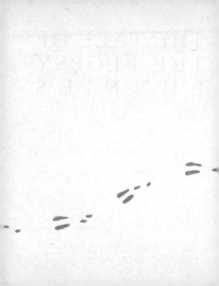

It is said that the effect of eating too much lettuce is "soporific."

I have never felt sleepy after eating lettuces; but then *I* am not a rabbit.

They certainly had a very soporific effect upon the Flopsy Bunnies!

When Benjamin Bunny grew up, he married his Cousin Flopsy. They had a large family, and they were very improvident and cheerful.

I do not remember the separate names of their children; they were generally called the

"Flopsy
Bunnies."

As there was not
always quite enough to
eat, Benjamin used to
borrow cabbages from
Flopsy's brother,

THE TALE OF THE FLOPSY BUNNIES

Peter Rabbit, who kept a
nursery garden.
Sometimes Peter

Rabbit had no cabbages
to spare.

When this happened,
the Flopsy Bunnies went
across the field to a rubbish
heap, in the ditch outside
Mr. McGregor's garden.

Mr. McGregor's rub-
bish heap was a mixture.
There were jam pots and
paper bags, and moun-

tains of chopped grass
from the mowing ma-
chine (which always
tasted oily), and some
rotten vegetable marrows
and an old boot or
two. One
day—oh joy!—
there were
a quantity
of over-

grown lettuces, which
had "shot" into flower.

The Flopsy Bunnies
simply stuffed lettuces.
By degrees, one after
another, they were over-
come with

slumber,

and lay down in the mown grass.

Benjamin was not so much overcome as his children. Before going to sleep he was sufficiently wide awake to put a paper bag over his head to keep off the flies.

The little Flopsy Bunnies slept delightfully in

the warm sun. From the
lawn beyond the garden
came the distant clack-
etty sound of the mowing
machine. The blue-bottles
buzzed about the wall,
and a little old mouse
picked over the rubbish
among the jam pots.

(I can tell you her
name, she was called

Thomasina Tittlemouse, a woodmouse with a long tail.)

She rustled across the paper bag, and awakened Benjamin Bunny.

The mouse apologized profusely, and said that she knew Peter Rabbit.

While she and Benjamin were talking, close under the wall, they heard a heavy tread above their heads; and suddenly Mr. McGregor emptied out a sackful of lawn mowings right upon the top of the sleeping Flopsy Bunnies! Benjamin shrank down under his paper bag. The mouse hid in a jam pot.

The little rabbits smiled sweetly in their sleep under the shower of grass; they did not awake because the lettuces had been so soporific.

They dreamt that their mother Flopsy was

tucking them up in a hay bed.

Mr. McGregor looked down after emptying his sack. He saw some funny little brown tips of ears sticking up through the lawn mowings. He stared at them for some time.

Presently a fly

settled on one of them and it moved.

Mr. McGregor climbed down on to the rubbish heap—

"One, two, three, four! five! six leetle rabbits!" said he as he dropped them into his sack. The Flopsy Bunnies dreamt that their mother

was turning them over in
bed. They stirred a little
in their sleep, but still
they did not wake up.

Mr. McGregor tied up
the sack and left it on the
wall.

He went to put
away the mow-
ing machine.
While he

was gone, Mrs. Flopsy Bunny (who had remained at home) came across the field.

She looked suspiciously at the sack and wondered where everybody was?

Then the mouse came out of her jam pot, and Benjamin took the paper bag off his head, and they told the doleful tale.

Benjamin and Flopsy were in despair; they could not undo the string.

But Mrs. Tittlemouse was a resourceful person. She nibbled a hole in the bottom corner of the sack.

The little rabbits were pulled out and pinched to wake them.

Their parents stuffed

the empty sack with
three rotten vegetable
marrows, an old blacking

brush and two decayed turnips.

Then they all hid under a bush and watched for Mr. McGregor.

Mr. McGregor came back and picked up the sack, and carried it off.

He carried it hanging down, as if it were rather heavy.

The Flopsy Bunnies followed at a safe distance.

They watched him go into his house.

And then they crept up

113

to the window to listen.

Mr. McGregor threw down the sack on the stone floor in a way that would have been extremely painful to the Flopsy Bunnies, if they had happened to have been inside it.

They could hear him drag his chair on the

flags, and chuckle—

"One, two, three, four, five, six leetle rabbits!" said Mr. McGregor.

115

"Eh? What's that? What have they been spoiling now?" enquired Mrs. McGregor.

"One, two, three, four, five, six leetle fat rabbits!" repeated Mr. McGregor, counting on his fingers—"one, two, three—"

"Don't you be silly;

what do you mean, you silly old man?"

"In the sack! one, two, three, four, five, six!" replied Mr. McGregor.

(The youngest Flopsy Bunny got upon the window-sill.)

Mrs. McGregor took hold of the sack and felt

it. She said she could feel
six, but they must be *old*
rabbits, because they
were so hard and all
different shapes.

"Not fit to eat; but the
skins will do fine to line
my old cloak."

"Line your old cloak?"
shouted Mr. McGregor—
"I shall sell them and

buy myself baccy!"

"Rabbit tobacco! I shall skin them and cut off their heads."

Mrs. McGregor untied the sack and put her hand inside.

When she felt the vegetables she became very very angry.

119

She said that Mr. McGregor had "done it a purpose."

And Mr. McGregor was very angry too. One of the rotten marrows came flying through the kitchen window, and hit the youngest

Flopsy Bunny.

It was rather hurt.

Then Benjamin and Flopsy thought that it was time to go home.

So Mr. McGregor did not get his tobacco, and Mrs. McGregor did not get her rabbit skins.

But next Christmas Thomasina Tittlemouse

got a present of enough
rabbit-wool to make
herself a cloak and a
hood, and a handsome
muff and
a pair of
warm
mittens.

Love: Quotations from the Heart

Love Sonnets of Shakespeare

Motherhood

The Night Before Christmas

Quotable Women

*Sherlock Holmes:
Two Complete Adventures*

Tales from the Arabian Nights

Tales of Peter Rabbit

The Velveteen Rabbit

The Wit and Wisdom of Mark Twain

Women's Wit and Wisdom

This book has been bound using
handcraft methods, and Smythe-sewn to
ensure durability.

The dust-jacket was designed by
Toby Schmidt.
The interior was designed
by Jacqueline Spadaro.
The interior and dust-jacket
illustrations are
by Charles Santore.
The text was typeset in
Century Schoolbook by
Commcor Communications Corporation,
Philadelphia, Pennsylvania.